W9-CHP-120

Picking Apples

SIMON SPOTLIGHT
An imprint of Simon & Schuster Children's Publishing Division
1230 Avenue of the Americas, New York, NY 10020
This Simon Spotlight edition August 2022
First Aladdin Paperbacks edition September 2009
Text copyright © 2009 by Brenda Bowen
Illustrations copyright © 2009 by Mike Gordon
For information about special discounts for bulk purchases, please contact
Simon & Schuster Special Sales at 1-866-506-1949 or business@simonandschuster.com.
Manufactured in the United States of America 0722 LAK
2 4 6 8 10 9 7 5 3 1
Library of Congress Cataloging-in-Publication Data
McNamara, Margaret.
Picking apples / by Margaret McNamara ;
illustrated by Mike Gordon. — 1st Aladdin ed.
p. cm. — (Ready-to-read) (Robin Hill School)
Summary: Michael refuses to help his classmates pick apples during a field trip until his
teacher, Mrs. Connor, finds the apple that is just right for him.
[1. Apples—Fiction. 2. School field trips—Fiction.] I. Gordon, Mike, 1948 Mar. 16– ill.
II. Title.
PZ7.M47879343Pic 2009
[E]—dc22
ISBN 978-1-6659-1999-9 (hc)
ISBN 978-1-4169-5539-9 (pbk)
ISBN 978-1-4169-8594-5 (ebook)

Robin Hill School

Picking Apples

Written by Margaret McNamara
Illustrated by Mike Gordon

Ready-to-Read

Simon Spotlight
New York   London   Toronto   Sydney   New Delhi

Mrs. Connor's class
went on a field trip.

"Time for some
apple picking,"
Mrs. Connor said.

"I will not pick apples," said Michael.

Eigen climbed up
a pointy ladder.

He pulled down
twelve red apples.
"One dozen!" he said.

Ayanna and Hannah
picked apples
off the ground.

They found ten green apples.
"My back hurts!"
said Hannah.

Eigen and Becky
shook a tree.

Four red-and-green
apples fell down.
"That was easy," said Eigen.

Nick and Emma jumped up
and picked seven
speckled apples each.

"Hard work!" said Nick.

Katie sat on the ground
and waited till apples
fell into her lap.

She got two golden
apples that way.
"No sweat," said Katie.

The apples were
piling up.

Michael added zero
apples to the pile.

"Did you know apples
have names?"
asked Mrs. Connor.

"That is an Idared,"
said Mrs. Connor.

"Yum!" said Eigen.

"This one is a Honeycrisp,

and this one is a Russet,

and that one is a Crispin," said Mrs. Connor.

"Crisp!" said Ayanna.

"Boring," said Michael.

"And this one is for you,
Michael,"
said Mrs. Connor.

"What?" said Michael.
"It is a Granny Smith,"
said Mrs. Connor.

"Smith?" said Michael.
"That is my name!
My name is Michael Smith."

"Now will you pick
some apples?"
asked Mrs. Connor.

"I pick this one!"
said Michael.
"The apple named for me!"